The Fisherman and his Wife

Written by Tanya Landman

Illustrated by Martina Peluso

Collins

There was once a fisherman and his wife who lived in a leaky little shed down by the sea.

Every day, the fisherman walked across the beach, sat himself down on a rock and did some fishing.

Every day, the fisherman's wife stayed at home, sat herself down in her chair and did some rocking.

3

One bright spring morning, the fisherman got
up early. The sun was rising in the east, sending shafts
of red and gold across the sky. The sea, lying flat as
a sheet of glass, reflected the sunrise like a mirror.

The fisherman sat himself down on his rock, dropped
his hook into the deep water and let out his fishing line.

He was staring up at the sky
when suddenly his fishing line
got tugged down so hard he
nearly fell off his rock.
He'd hooked something big!

He hauled and heaved
and heaved and hauled
and finally, from
the depths
of the sea,
he pulled up …

5

… an enormous, fat, flat flounder. It was the biggest fish he'd ever seen.

Well, he was a fisherman and this was a fish. He was going to kill it.

But then the flounder looked at the fisherman with its beady blue eyes, opened its mouth and spoke! "Please don't hurt me," it said. "I'm not really a fish. I'm an enchanted prince."

"An enchanted prince?" said the fisherman. "Goodness me! Well of course I shall release you right away. It wouldn't be right to eat an enchanted prince."

He took his knife, cut the line and freed the flounder.
It dived back to the depths, leaving a streak of blood,
drawn like a red line through the water.

Scratching his head, the fisherman went home and told his wife.

She stopped rocking for a moment. She had a long think and then she said, "That flounder must've been a magic one. You should've asked that fish for a wish!"

"A wish?" chuckled the fisherman. "What would I wish for?"

The fisherman's wife looked at the leaky little shed. The rain dripped through the roof in the winter, and the wind poked its fingers through the cracks in the walls.

"Go and call him. Tell that fish I want a nice, cosy cottage," she said.

9

So the fisherman went back down to the sea.

He was surprised to see that the water had turned
a sickly-looking, greenish yellow. The wind was
whipping it into little waves.

Putting his hands up to his mouth,
the fisherman called:
"*Fat, flat flounder – magic fish,*
My old wife, she wants a wish."

Up came the fish from the depths of the sea.
"What does she want?" it asked.

"She wondered if you might give us a cottage,"
the fisherman replied.

"Go back home, fisherman," said the flounder.
"She's got what she asked for."

The fisherman went back home and there – instead of the leaky little shed – was a cosy cottage with a thatched roof. Pink and white roses were winding around the door. There were chickens pecking in the yard. Apple trees hung heavy with fruit, and vegetables grew in the garden.

The fisherman's wife had got exactly what she wished for. But was she happy? She was not.

The very next morning, she called her husband. "If that flounder could give us a cottage with just one flick of his tail, I think he could manage something a bit bigger. Go and call him. Tell that fish I want a mighty, magnificent castle."

Grumbling to himself a little, the fisherman went
back down to the sea. He was startled to see that
now the water had turned blue and purple, the colour
of a bruise. The wind had grown stronger and
the waves were bigger.

Putting his hands up to his mouth,
the fisherman called:
"Fat, flat flounder – magic fish,
My old wife, she wants a wish."

Up came the fish from the depths of the sea. "What does she want now?" it asked.

"She wants something bigger," the fisherman said with a sad sigh. "She wondered if you might give us a castle."

"Go back home, fisherman," said the flounder. "She's got what she asked for."

The fisherman went back home. Instead of a cosy little cottage, there was a mighty, magnificent castle with a moat and a drawbridge and four tall towers. Four staircases wound up and round and up and round to massive battlements.

It took the fisherman a very long time to find his wife.

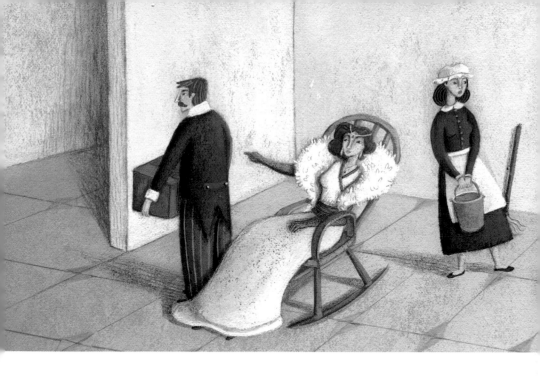

When he did, she was sitting in the great hall.
There were servants scurrying in every direction,
obeying her orders.

"Fetch this!" "Take that!" "Do this!" "Do that!"
"Scrub this!" "Wash that!"

The fisherman's wife had got exactly what she
wished for. But was she happy? She was not.

The very next morning, she called her husband.
"I don't see the point of living in a castle unless
I can be queen. Go and call him. Tell that fish I
want to be queen."

Muttering to himself and tutting under his breath, the fisherman went back down to the sea. He was alarmed to see that the water had turned as black as coal and the wind was blowing white crests on to huge waves.

Putting his hands up to his mouth,
the fisherman called:
"Fat, flat flounder – magic fish,
My old wife, she wants a wish."

Up came the fish from the depths of the sea.
"What does she want now?" it asked.

"She wants to be queen," the fisherman
said sorrowfully.

"Go back home, fisherman," sighed the flounder.
"She's got what she asked for."

The fisherman went back home.

There were royal flags flying from the castle towers. Soldiers in smart red uniforms marched up and down in the castle courtyard. Officers sat on prancing horses yelling commands: "Left, right, left, right! HALT!"

The fisherman's wife was in the great hall, but she wasn't in her rocking chair any more. She was sitting on a silver throne, wearing a red velvet cape trimmed with white fur.

On her head was a golden crown, studded with emeralds and rubies and sapphires and diamonds.

The fisherman's wife had got exactly what she wished for. But was she happy? She was not.

The fisherman's wife watched the sun set on the western side of the great hall. She sat on her silver throne all night.

In the morning, she watched the sun rise on the eastern side of the great hall. And then she called her husband.

"I want to be the one who tells the sun when it's time to go down. I want to be the one who tells the sun when it's time to come up. And the moon, too. It's not allowed to move, unless I give it permission. I want to be in charge of everything. Go and call him. Tell that fish I want to be Queen of the Universe."

"No!" protested the fisherman. "I can't! I won't!"

"I'M THE QUEEN," screamed the fisherman's wife, "AND YOU'RE NOBODY! I GIVE THE ORDERS! YOU GO DOWN TO THE SEA RIGHT NOW! CALL HIM! TELL THAT FISH I WANT TO BE QUEEN OF THE UNIVERSE!"

23

Grumbling to himself under his breath, the fisherman went back down to the sea. "This is wrong!" he mumbled. "All wrong. Wrong, wrong, wrong!"

The water was now scarlet and the sight of it terrified him. The whole sea seemed to be full of blood. Rain fell in sheets from great black clouds. Thunder roared and lightning tore the sky apart. The wind howled through monstrous waves that crashed on to the beach.

Putting his hands up to his mouth,
the fisherman yelled:
"Fat, flat flounder – magic fish,
My old wife, she wants a wish."

Up came the fish from the depths of the sea. "Now what?" it demanded.

The fisherman was so embarrassed, he could hardly speak. "My old wife," he said in a scared whisper, "she wants … she wants … she wants to be Queen of the Universe."

The fish looked at the fisherman and the fisherman looked at the fish. Both of them were silent for a long time.

But then the flounder growled, "Go back home, fisherman. She's got what she deserves."

The fisherman trudged miserably home across the beach, his heart as heavy as his feet. He was so petrified of what he might find that he held his hands over his eyes. He couldn't bear to look.

When at last he peered between his fingers, he saw …

No soldiers. No servants. No silver throne, no velvet robe, no golden crown. No mighty, magnificent castle. Not even a cosy cottage.

There was just the leaky little shed. And the fisherman's wife, sitting in her chair, doing some rocking.

And – maybe, just maybe – doing some thinking, too.

Be careful what you wish for

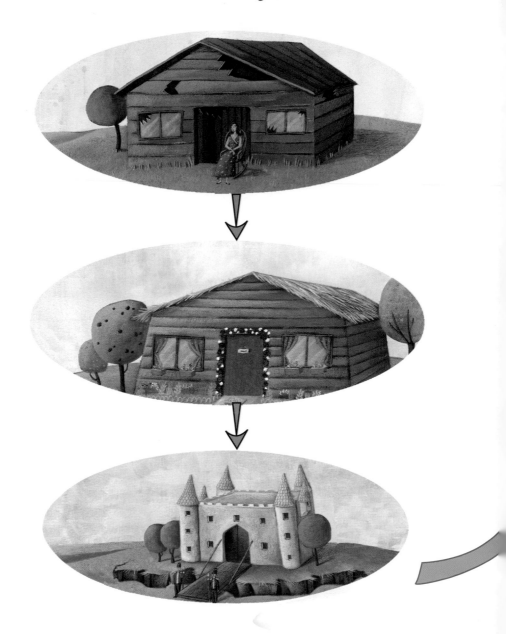

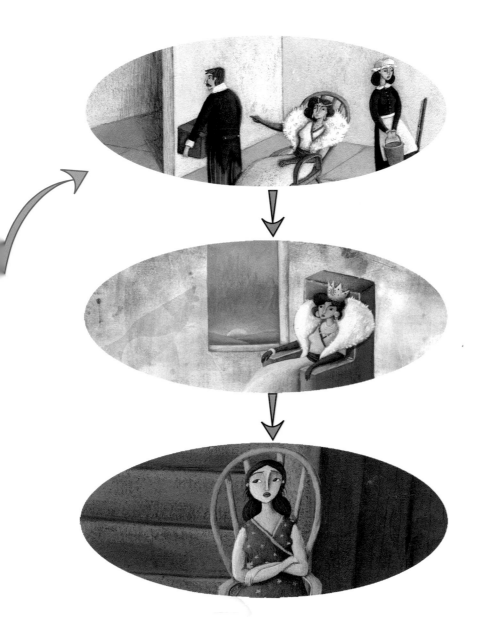

Ideas for reading

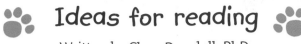

Written by Clare Dowdall, PhD
Lecturer and Primary Literacy Consultant

Reading objectives:
- draw inferences and justify these with evidence
- make predictions from details stated and applied
- identify main ideas drawn from more than one paragraph and summarise ideas

Spoken language objectives:
- participate in discussions, presentations, performances, role play, improvisations and debates

Curriculum links: PSHE – health and wellbeing: choices

Resources: art materials; pens and paper; ICT

Build a context for reading

- Look at the front cover and read the title. Ask children to suggest what the fisherman is thinking and what they can deduce about him.
- Read the blurb together. Ask children what they'd ask for if a magic creature offered to grant them a wish.
- Discuss what might happen to the fisherman and his wife, based on children's previous experiences of traditional tales.

Understand and apply reading strategies

- Ask children to take turns to read aloud to p7. Support them to read with expression, taking account of the punctuation.
- Pause at p7 and ask children what they can deduce about the fisherman's character, and what they'd have done in his situation.
- Ask children to read pp8–9 with a partner, and discuss what they can deduce about the fisherman's wife and what will happen next.
- Share ideas and ask children to read on to the end of the story to find out if the fisherman's wife gets her wish.